LEGO NINJAGO
Masters of Spinjitzu

A NINJA'S PATH

ADAPTED BY TRACEY WEST

SCHOLASTIC INC.
NEW YORK   TORONTO   LONDON   AUCKLAND
SYDNEY   MEXICO CITY   NEW DELHI   HONG KONG

ISBN 978-0-545-43593-2

12 11 10 9 8 7 6 5 4 3 2 1   12 13 14 15 16 17/0
Printed in the U.S.A.   40
First printing, June 2012

PREPARING FOR THE ENEMY

High in his mountain dojo, Sensei Wu was thinking about the Serpentine army. The snake creatures, led by Lloyd Garmadon, were a threat to Ninjago.

Luckily, Sensei Wu's ninja had taken the Serpentine general's staff. With the staff, the ninja could fight the effects of the Serpentine's hypnotic powers.

Up on the rooftop, Kai, Cole, Jay, and Zane were training. Each ninja had one of the Golden Weapons of Spinjitzu. Jay's Nunchuks spit out electric sparks. Kai's Sword blazed with fire. Cole swung his powerful Scythe.

Zane meditated quietly. Then he jumped up and began to spin. His Shurikens of Ice froze the whole rooftop!

"It's like Zane's in his own world," Jay complained.

"Sensei, Zane's weird," Kai told their teacher as he entered the room.

"What is weird?" Sensei asked. "Someone who is different, or someone who is different from *you*?"

"No, Sensei. He's *weird* weird," Cole insisted.

"Like when we watched that sad movie —
and he laughed!" Jay said.

"Or the time he started grooming himself
in the bathroom!" Cole complained. "Right in
front of me! Like I wasn't even there!"

"We like the guy," Kai said. "He's really smart. He's just a little . . . off sometimes."

"Zane is a brother, and brothers are often different," Sensei Wu told him. His face darkened as he thought of his own brother, the evil Lord Garmadon. "I should know."

A gong rang out.

"Mail!" cried Kai, Jay, and Cole. They ran to get their letters and packages. But there was nothing for Zane.

"Hey, Zane . . . how come you don't ever hear from your parents?" Jay asked.

"I don't remember my parents," Zane replied. "I've been an orphan all my life."

A SERPENTINE SPY

Cole opened a package for his dragon, Rocky — a tasty toad. As he fed Rocky, someone was watching — through Cole's own eyes!

The watcher was a Serpentine named Scales. He had hypnotized Cole during a battle in Jamanakai Village. Now he could see everything Cole saw.

The Serpentine soldiers were busy building a tree house for Lloyd Garmadon. Scales thought it was a silly idea.

"I must question *thisss* childish agenda," he told the general. "The ninja have our staff. We should get it back."

"How dare you question me?" demanded the general.

A NIGHT VISITOR

Back at the dojo, it was Zane's turn to cook.

"Dinner is served!" he announced.

When the other ninja caught sight of him, they all laughed. Zane was wearing a frilly pink apron.

"What's so funny?" Zane asked. He didn't think it was strange at all.

"Well, how about this?" Cole asked. He mashed his plate of food in Kai's face. "Now *that's* funny!"

Then Sensei Wu dumped his food on top of Cole's head. A food fight started. Everyone laughed and joined in — except for Zane.

That night, Zane looked up at the stars.

Is this the place I really belong? he wondered.

A falcon landed on a tree branch near Zane. Zane shook his head, and the bird shook its head. Zane flapped his arms, and the bird flapped his wings. Who was this strange new friend?

Zane followed the falcon into the forest. The bird led him to the Serpentine's fort. Then it flew off into the night.

MISSION: TREE HOUSE

Zane ran and got his friends. The four ninja raced through the forest.

"So, tell us again how you found Lloyd's secret headquarters?" Kai asked.

"I followed a bird," Zane explained.

The ninja laughed — until they saw that Zane was right.

"It looks like those three trees are holding up the whole thing," Kai said. "Once we untie the ropes, the whole thing will fall."

The four ninja sneaked into the fort and spied on Lloyd.

"You! Hold up that sign for me!" Lloyd yelled at one of the snake soldiers.

The soldier held up a sign that read, "No Girls or Ninja."

The ninja split up. Jay raced to one of the ropes holding up the fort.

"Ninjago!" he yelled. Then he twirled, using Spinjitzu to cut through the rope.

"Ninjago!" Zane took down the second rope. The fort began to fall apart.

"I said NO ninja!" Lloyd yelled. "Attack!"

"Cole, wait until we're out of the fort. Then cut the last line!" Kai called.

Cole nodded. But Scales saw him.

"You are under my command," he hissed.

Scales ordered Cole to fight the other ninja. Then he raised his scaly fist in the air. "Now to get the staff!"

The tree house swayed back and forth. But the ninja couldn't jump off. They were too busy fighting Cole!

"Friends don't hit friends," Jay said.

But Cole attacked them with the Scythe of Quakes.

The others didn't want to hurt him. Jay used his Nunchuks of Lightning to try to shock Cole out of his trance.

Bam! The lightning hit Cole. Cole bounced back to his feet, angry. He pushed Jay off the tree house.

Then Cole ran to the last rope and raised his Scythe. Once he cut the rope, the tree house — and all the ninja — would fall.

"No, Cole!" Jay, Kai, and Zane cried.

Suddenly, the sound of a flute filled the air. Cole put down the scythe.

It was Sensei Wu! He and Nya flew to the rescue on Kai's dragon.

"That flute cancels their powers!" Jay realized.

"Where am I?" Cole asked. "What are we doing?"

"We're getting out of here because this whole place is coming down!" Nya warned.

The four ninja jumped onto the dragon. *Boom!* The tree house crashed to the ground.

"We must hurry!" Sensei Wu said. "The dojo is unguarded!"

RAIDED!

But they were too late. The dojo was in flames!

Kai made a fist. "Those snakes!"

The dragons were trapped in the burning stable. Cole quickly pulled a lever and set them free.

Zane called to his dragon. "Shard! Put this out!"

Shard blasted the flames with his icy breath. The fire went out, but it was too late.

Kai looked around at the ruins. "Our home," he said sadly. "It's all gone."

Kai, Jay, and Cole were angry with Zane. "If you hadn't followed that silly bird, none of this would have happened!" Kai yelled.

"Enough!" Sensei Wu cried. "Zane is your brother. Say you are sorry."

But when the boys turned around, Zane was gone.

THE SLITHER PIT

The Serpentine stole the staff from the dojo. Then they went back to their icy underground tomb. Scales proudly held the staff.

"Give me back my staff!" the general demanded.

"No," Scales said. "We will have to fight for it — in the Slither Pit!"

A soldier took the staff from Scales. "Winner gets the staff and leads the tribe!" he yelled. "There are no rules. Now fight!"

Weapons made of ice lowered from the ceiling. The general grabbed a shield and an axe. Scales grabbed two swords.

"Go, General!" Lloyd yelled.

The general whipped his long tail at Scales. But Scales used fang-kwon-do.

"*Hii-yaaa!*" He kicked the general in the chin, and the general fell back. He couldn't get up. Scales had won!

A soldier handed the staff to Scales. His feet began to glow. They turned into a long blue tail. Scales was the general now!

"Scales! Scales! Scales!" the Serpentine shouted.

The old general's tail turned into legs.

"You will be loyal to *me* now!" Scales told him. Then he turned to Lloyd. "Leave and never return!"

The snakes left Lloyd outside in the frozen wilderness. But before he left, he stole their map.

A NEW HOME

Back at the mountain, Cole, Jay, Kai, Nya, and Sensei Wu huddled around a fire. They were cold and tired — and eating mud newt for dinner.

"We must be thankful for what we still have," Sensei Wu reminded them.

"What do we have?" Cole asked. "We don't have our home."

"I don't miss our home," Kai said. "I miss Zane."

Just then, Zane came walking up the mountain.

"Zane, we're so sorry for everything we said!" Jay said.

"Why?" Zane asked. "That is not why I left. I saw the falcon again. Come, let me show you what I have found."

"I feel a strange connection with that falcon,"
Zane explained as they walked. "I think he is
trying to show us the path we need to take."
  They walked over a hill, and then they saw it
— a deserted ship. It looked warm and cozy.
  "Do I smell pie?" Jay asked.
  Zane smiled. "Yes. I made dinner."

The ninja let out a cheer and ran to the ship.

"Thank you, Zane," Sensei Wu said. "One day, we will find your family."

"I've already found them," Zane replied. He smiled and looked at his friends.